The Autumn Visitors by Karel Hayes

Joyce
"Let's have a turkey-less Thanksgiving."
Janicki

Published by Down East Books
An imprint of The Rowman & Littlefield Publishing Group, Inc.
4501 Forbes Boulevard, Suite 200, Lanham, Maryland 20706
www.rowman.com

Unit A, Whitacre Mews, 26-34 Stannary Street, London SE11 4AB, United Kingdom

Distributed by
NATIONAL BOOK NETWORK
1-800-462-6420

British Library Cataloguing in Publication Information Available

Library of Congress Cataloging-in-Publication Data Available
ISBN 978-1-60893-454-6 (cloth)
eISBN 978-1-60893-455-3 (electronic)

The paper used in this publication meets the minimum requirements of American National Standard for Information Sciences—
Permanence of Paper for Printed Library Materials, ANSI/NISO Z39.48-1992.

Printed in the United States of America

Columbus Day weekend is here;

they can go to the cottage

and visit a fair.

The leaves will be falling,

the air will be cool,

but the cottage is cozy —

a fire in the hearth and games

to be played.

It's only a weekend and too soon time to leave,

but the cottage by the water will not be empty for long.

Halloween is the most fun fall holiday,

with pumpkins and costumes

and trick-or-treating to do.

Then it's on to Thanksgiving —

catching a turkey

and making

the very best meal;

so all can be thankful

for another year.